This is a story about a journey.

Grey has lost her mother and her faith, and she is struggling to make sense of the world. As she continues to struggle and ask questions, she finds answers in the people she encounters and the places she never expected to go.

This is a story about people just like you and me.

We all go through challenging times. Life is difficult, and it is especially tough when it feels like we are going through those times alone.

This is a story about learning, growing, and connecting.

Every day is an opportunity to learn something new, to expand the way we think, and to re-examine or reinforce our view of the world. If it helps you on your journey, then it has been a success.

Dear Reader,

This is the place where famous and not-so-famous people tell you how much they like this book.

Well, this time, I would like to hear from YOU. I have dedicated the space on the following page to you. Please write down your thoughts and impressions and then email them to me at info@skipcarney.com. You can also text or call me at 252.813.1303. I would really love to hear from you.

If you feel inclined, share your thoughts with your friends and family. Post comments on your social media channels or write a review on Amazon or Good Reads or wherever you see book reviews.

I hope you find valuable lessons in this book that encourage you on your journey. Please share it with someone you love. Love is one of God's greatest gifts. The more you give away, the more you get back.

Thank you.

Skip Carney
Be the light.

Your Notes

The Greatest Disciple in the World
Copyright ©2024 by Earl Burton Carney, Jr., and the Foundation for Christian Education. All rights reserved. Except for brief quotations in critical articles or reviews, no part of this text may be reproduced, transmitted, downloaded, decompiled, reverse-engineered, or stored in or introduced into any information storage and retrieval system in any form or by any means, whether electronic or mechanical without the express written permission of the author, Skip Carney, or publisher, the Foundation for Christian Education.

© February 2024: ISBN 978-1-7326373-2-0

Requests for information should be addressed to:
Foundation for Christian Education, P.O. Box 7398, Rocky Mount, NC 27804, or info@skipcarney.com.

All Scripture quotations, unless otherwise indicated, are taken from the Holy Bible, NIV, or NLT versions.

The "NIV" and "New International Version" are trademarks registered in the United States Patent and Trademark Office by Biblica, Inc.™ New International Version®, NIV®. Copyright ©1973, 1978, 1984, 2011 by Biblica, Inc.™ Used by permission of Zondervan. www.zondervan.com. All rights reserved worldwide.

Scripture quotations marked (NLT) are taken from the Holy Bible, New Living Translation, copyright ©1996, 2004, 2015 by Tyndale House Foundation. Used by permission of Tyndale House Publishers, Inc., Carol Stream, Illinois 60188. All rights reserved.

The Greatest Disciple in the World

by Skip Carney

Acknowledgments

This book has been five years in the making. It has taken many twists and turns along the way and surprised me in many ways. When I completed the first draft, I quickly realized that it still had a way to go before it would be called "finished."

Along the way, I have received help and encouragement from friends, family, and clergy. In the early days, my friend Bob Manning asked what this book would be about. When I told him, he was the one who said, "No, no, you're not going to make a disciple out of *me!* I'm not disciple material." My C12 friends have patiently encouraged me, and I am grateful for their faith and friendship.

Pastors Chris Aiken and Richard Gurganus were gracious in helping me understand discipleship in simple terms and pointing me in the direction of resources that helped clarify my own understanding. Chris was among the editorial review team that gave me great feedback on the first draft. That team included my wife Karen, my daughter Spencer Grace, and friends Daniel Whiteman and Robert Beaman. Each gave me valuable insight and direction that provided the guidance I needed to complete the "final" draft. Thank you all.

I should also credit the late Oswald Chambers. Of all the material I read on the Sermon on the Mount, his account made the most sense to me and connected all the dots. His book is called *Studies in the Sermon on the Mount*.

The Foundation for Christian Education

All proceeds from the sale of this book go directly to the Foundation for Christian Education, a 501(c)(3) not-for-profit organization. The purpose of the foundation is to develop, promote, and implement Christian educational content and materials for students of all ages.

To order bulk quantities of this book, study guides, Beacon Booklets, Be the Light window decals, and to join our email list, visit:

www.foundationforchristianeducation.com

Dedication

This book is dedicated to my wife, Karen, and daughters Jessica, Kathryn, and Spencer Grace. And to the many family, friends, and strangers who read *The Greatest Church in the World* and have patiently waited for this book to arrive.

The Greatest Disciple in the World

Be the Light

by Skip Carney

One of the men lying there had been sick for thirty-eight years. When Jesus saw him and knew he had been ill for a long time, he asked him, "Would you like to get well?"
John 5:5-6 (NLT)

Chapter One

Grey stared into the light. She felt the burn in the back of her skull. The pain was unbearable, but she couldn't stop staring. She was lying on a bean bag on the floor of Alex's apartment. Alex stepped into the light.

"Why is there a halo around you?" she slurred.

"There's no halo, dummy. You're blitzed."

"Are you God? You look like God."

"Shut up."

"Why am I here, God? Why? I just don't understand."

And she passed out. Grey was 19, but the circles under her eyes and the defeated look on her face conveyed a sadder, older person. As she drifted in and out of consciousness, she dreamed of the young girl she used to know. Life was full of dreams then. Full of laughter and love. Back then, she talked to God a lot. She talked about becoming a dancer, a scientist, or a pilot. She could hear God laugh as she bounced from one dream to another. She always thought He was laughing with her. Now, it seemed He was laughing at her. She was destined for nothing, going nowhere, and was getting there fast. She opened her eyes. The light was blinding.

She squinted. "Where's the wine?"

"You've had enough."

"Gimme the bottle, Turkey," she demanded.

Alex turned and walked into the kitchen. Turkey was her pet name for him. He tolerated it, but he didn't really like it. Alex was in his early 20s. He had a small apartment on the edge of town and let Grey crash there when she needed to 'get away' when the world was closing in on her. His hair was the color of sand and moved in slow motion as he laughed and flung his head back to get it out of his eyes. Grey liked those eyes. *Two wells of kindness in a world of hurt,* she called them.

"Why are you so mean to me?" She cried.

"Ha! I'm your best friend."

"You're my *only* friend, Turkey."

"Makes me your best friend, right?"

"You win. Pass the bottle."

"Nope. You're outta here. Your old man will be looking for you," Alex said, throwing a coat in her direction. "Go!"

"Why are you so mean to me?"

"Cause I love you, dummy. Go home. Be careful. Get some sleep. Tomorrow will be better."

"You always say that."

Alex held her coat as she struggled to stand and slip it on.

"Grey."

"What? Is it on backwards?"

"No. I want to talk to you for a minute."

"I thought you were kicking me out."

"Listen. This is not working."

"I like this coat."

"Not the coat dummy. I'm serious. You've been trying to drown your grief for years now. I thought I was helping, but clearly, I'm not."

"I don't think I like you being serious."

"I've been going to church lately."

"Whoa. That is serious."

"Actually, it has been … well, it's been liberating."

"No way."

"I went in for the first time last spring. It's the Lighthouse. The little church downtown."

"You can stop right there. I'm not ready for church."

"Grey, you've lost your mom, but you still have Ray. You have your life. It would be a shame to go on living it like this. I don't think your mother would want that."

"You're right. You aren't helping."

Grey stepped into the cold night air. Her long, brown hair flew into her face as the wind attacked from out of nowhere. She tucked the unruly strands under her toboggan and marched into the night. *Even the wind hates me,* she thought. *It was another pointless end to another meaningless day.* Her stepfather would be waiting. Patiently. Ironically. She sure didn't deserve his patience or his presence. *Why does he stick around? Why does he care?*

She used to love her stepdad. He was a great guy. He worked hard and took care of Grey and her mom. And her mother had adored him. Grey's dad died when she was very young, and Ray stepped in to pick up the pieces. He worked with his hands, and to everyone else, he was the best mechanic in the county. To Grey, he was the reason her mom was gone. Five years ago, he had fixed the brakes on her car. Five years ago today, she was alive and on the way to pick Grey up from school for piano practice. She crashed on the way. She didn't survive.

Every year since Grey had found her way to Alex's to try to drink away the anniversary of that day. To erase the memory and the pain. It didn't help.

Grey stopped and leaned against a lamp post. Tears were streaming down her face. "Why? Why?" She screamed into the night. "She was one of the good ones. She loved you, God. Is that why you took her? You needed company?" She sat on the curb until there were no more tears to cry. Just the old, now-familiar anger she felt whenever she thought of her mom.

"Take me," she yelled. "Take me from this place."

She found her way home and fell into bed. *Maybe I won't wake up,* she thought.

The following day, Grey was awakened by a knock on her bedroom door. "Abigail, we need to talk," it was her stepdad. He never knocked on her door, he never called her Abigail, and they never talked. *Must be serious,* she thought.

"Don't call me Abigail," she yelled. "I'll, uh, I'll be there in a minute." She struggled to get the words out. Her mom used to call her Abigail. Abigail Greyson when she was ticked about something. After her mom died, she switched to Grey and told everyone that Abigail was dead.

Ray was standing in the kitchen as she shuffled in. His strong, ruddy face had more than a hint of worry on it. She had seen sadness, disappointment, anger, and pain in that face. She had never seen worry.

"What's up?" she queried, reaching for a piece of toast. "Is this the 'college' talk again?"

"No. That ship has sailed, Grey." He never looked up. His eyes were fixed on the floor.

"I might go next year," she said half-heartedly. Even she knew she was lying.

"You've got to go to work," he said. He was still staring at the floor.

"Work? No way."

"Grey, it's not optional. It's my hands. I … it's the arthritis."

She looked at his hands. The hands that had held her bike when she learned to ride. The hands that had held hers and taught her how to dance. The hands that her mom loved to hold, though they were always stained with grease. The hands that had turned wrenches for over 30 years.

"I need surgery," tears were welling in his eyes. "The doctors say I might not be able to work again. Surgery is my only hope."

"Don't expect sympathy from me," Grey said without thinking. "I mean …"

"I've talked to my friend at the coffee shop downtown. He needs some help, and he says he will train you."

"I don't want to work at a coffee shop."

"It's not work if you love it," Ray offered.

"I'm not going to love it."

"We'll see," Ray paused for a second as he re-focused on Grey. "My surgery is tomorrow. You start work today."

"Today? I have plans."

"He wants to see you at 2. It's the Barnabas Coffee Shop. Don't be late. Ask for Nick."

God blesses those who are merciful, for they will be shown mercy.

Matthew 5:7 (NLT)

Chapter Two

"I won't be here long," Grey announced as she entered the coffee shop. "Just until Ray gets back to work."

Nick laughed. "I'm Nick. Ray told me you would be 'interesting.' Glad you could make it in. Ever worked in a coffee shop before?"

Silence.

"I'll take that as a no." Nick allowed a few seconds to pass. "Do you like coffee?"

"I don't hate it," came the reply.

"Okay. We'll start there. Here's a cup." She took it with a grunt. Undaunted, Nick spent the next three hours showing Grey the ropes of the Barnabas Coffee Shop. It was eclectic, with a wild collection of sofas, tables, and chairs. Nooks for meetings. Nooks for reading or working from a laptop. Nick supported local artists, so the walls were adorned with watercolors, pastels, and oil paintings of people, places, and things. Wednesday was open mic night when local musicians would come by to try out new songs or their versions of old pop hits.

"What is a Barnabas?" asked Grey.

"Who."

"What?"

"Who," Nick repeated.

"Who's on first?" Grey grinned.

They both laughed.

"Laughter sounds good on you," he said. "I'd like to hear it more."

Grey blushed. "Seriously, what's Barnabas?"

"Barnabas isn't a what. He was a who from the Bible. He was famous for helping the apostle Paul during his trials and travels. He was strong in his faith despite the consequences. And Barnabas means 'comfort' in Hebrew." Nick added, "We want this place to be a place to make friends and find comfort. Maybe even help each other."

"What consequences?"

"He was killed for his faith."

"Might not want to put that on the billboard," she said. Grey made a rectangle with her fingers, the way a movie director does when trying to picture the scene. "I can see it now ... 'Coffee to Die For' ... get it while it's hot."

"Funny. I was thinking about adding those exact words to the menu board."

They laughed again.

"Hey, what's with the sticker on the window?"

"What sticker?" Nick glanced towards the window.

"The one that says 'Forgiveness is Here' with the little lighthouse."

"Oh, that. It's a message from the Lighthouse Church."

"Okay."

"Like I said, we want to help each other here. Sometimes we need to forgive. Sometimes we need to be forgiven. We have Bible verses and encouraging signs all over the place.."

"Jesus forgives," she added.

"Right."

"No matter what?"

"Well. It's kind of unconditionally conditional... or maybe conditionally unconditional."

"What?"

"If you ask God for forgiveness, you will receive it. That's the unconditional part."

"What's the catch? The condition?"

"You have to ask for it, and you have to choose to follow Jesus. Follow his teachings. Love God. Love others. Stuff like that."

"I used to believe. Now, I'm not so sure."

"Why?"

"Exactly. Why? Why would the God who loves me take my mother?"

"Yeah. That's a tough one."

Grey looked around the coffee shop. It was the slowest time of the day. There were a couple of people working on their laptops. A businessman was talking on his phone in the corner. Otherwise, it was quiet. She felt a tear start down her cheek.

"I miss her so much."

Nick was silent for a moment. "Do you think she's in Heaven?"

"I don't know. We hadn't been to church in a while. Not since I was a child." Grey was staring at the sign in the window. "Forgiveness..." she breathed.

"Maybe you should ..."

Grey interrupted. "What did Jesus say about forgiveness?"

"A lot." Nick put a finger to his temple. "He said to forgive your enemies. Anyone who has wronged you. He said to forgive …"

"What if the person you need to forgive is not your enemy and never wronged you?"

"Maybe you need to forgive yourself. We can all use a little forgiveness now and then, can't we?"

"I guess we all can." Grey grabbed her coat. "I've been such an idiot. Look, Nick. I can't do this."

"I, uh, understand."

"I mean. I can't do this today." Grey looked lost for words. "My dad is having surgery tomorrow, and I need to be there. I'll be here the next day if that's okay."

"We start making coffee at 5."

"AM?"

"Yep."

"I'll see you then." And she was gone just like that.

"Funny girl," Nick smiled. "Really funny."

The door flung open again. It was Grey.

"And Nick … Thank you."

"You're welcome."

Be the Light

The Greatest Disciple in the World

Above all, clothe yourselves with love, which binds us all together in perfect harmony.

Colossians 3:14 (NLT)

Chapter Three

The hospital room was like every hospital room she'd ever seen. The smell of pain and sickness hung in the air like a dark cloud. It made her shiver when she first entered the building, but she was used to it after a couple of hours. She was sitting in the faux leather chair next to the bed where Ray was sleeping. The doctor said the surgery had gone well but took twice as long as planned. "The arthritis was more extensive than we originally thought," he said with a shrug. "He is in God's hands now," the doctor said.

"It's not God's hands I am worried about," she said out loud.

"Don't worry, baby, my hands will be fine." It was Ray. Half awake.

"You haven't called me 'baby' … for a long time," she said.

"Sorry … I"

"It's okay. I like it. I've missed it."

"I wasn't sure you would be here."

"Ray … Dad … I need to tell you something." Grey held her breath. Ray waited. "I'm sorry. I'm really, really sorry. I have been a total jerk the past five years …"

"I understand …"

"No. You don't."

"Grey. I do understand." She stood up and moved toward the bed. Tears welled in her eyes. "Baby, I forgive you."

She blurted. "When mom died, I blamed you. You had just worked on her car, so it must have been your fault. When I saw the guilt in your eyes, I knew you also felt the blame."

"I know," he said. "And when you needed me most, I was lost in self-pity and guilt, and I just wasn't there for you."

"And I forgive you. I couldn't ease your pain, and I only made it worse. Even so, somehow, some way, you never gave up on me," she said.

"I love you, Grey. Always have. Always will. And I've missed you."

She looked at him, and at that moment, she saw the dad she knew before the crash. She reached to hug him. He reached for her.

"Ouch! Ouch! Hands!"

Through tears, they laughed out loud and found a way to hug without bumping into Ray's heavily bandaged hands.

They sat in silence for a while. She thought he was asleep. He opened his eyes and said, "She's in Heaven, you know."

"She's what? ... wait. How do you know?"

"She called me that day. She was at church."

And then he fell asleep again. The nurse said he would sleep through the night. "We gave him enough painkillers to knock out a horse," she laughed. "Go home and get some rest yourself."

"Must be the drugs talking." She sat silently for a moment, and as the nurse was about to leave the room, it hit her. "But … Rest?" She exclaimed. "I've got to be at work tomorrow at 5. What time do you go to bed when you have to work at 5?"

"AM? Soon, dear. Soon."

Grey kissed Ray on the cheek and whispered good night. As she left the hospital, she saw a placard on the table in the waiting room. It read 'Heal Here.' It had a small lighthouse in the corner.

That little lighthouse is everywhere, she thought. *Funny, I never noticed before. Tomorrow, I'm going to be at Barnabas. I've been a pain in the butt for too long. Tomorrow, I start helping. Tomorrow will be better.*

On the way home, she called Alex. "You're never gonna see me again," she exclaimed.

"Never? What do you mean?"

"Well. Not never. Just never like *that*. Like you've seen me. You've been a good, patient friend, but I will no longer need your bean bag or wine."

"What changed?"

"I just realized how stupid I've been. Ray is all I've got. You were right."

"He's not *all* you've got."

"Well, and you, of course."

"And God, Grey. You do have God."

"Yeah. I'm gonna work on that."

"Awesome."

"Hey, I'm starting a job at the coffee shop. You should come by."

"If I have time. I, um. I'm leaving town."

"Wait. You're what?"

"I was going to call. I am going to school. I just got the letter today."

"Turkey."

"Ha! Don't worry. I'll be back."

"Sure you will."

"I promise."

"And 'tomorrow will be better,'" they said in unison.

Be the Light

The Greatest Disciple in the World

Work at living in peace with everyone...
Hebrews 12:14 (NLT)

Chapter Four

Grey was at the coffee shop early.

"Sure is dark this time of day."

"You'll get used to it," Nick said as he wiped the counter. "We make our own light here," he said with a wink.

"What do you mean?"

"Nobody comes here just for coffee, Grey. You'll see."

The front door opened, and it began—the steady flow of bleary-eyed businesspeople, students, doctors, and police officers. The place warmed up as the patrons entered, and the chatter picked up. It seemed to brighten, too. It glowed as if generating light.

"I thought the light thing was a metaphor," she said between guests.

"It is," Nick smiled. "But it's real, too. Just look around."

"How's Ray?" asked one businessman. "I heard he had surgery."

"Uh, he's great. Thanks." She turned to Nick, "Who are these people? I don't know anyone, but they seem to know Ray. That's the third person to ask about him."

"Your dad has worked on almost every car in that parking lot. Everybody does know Ray." Nick studied Grey. "They know you, too."

"My reputation precedes me?"

"Something like that." He grinned. "Let's just say your mom touched a lot of souls in this town. Your dad has made many friends, and many people have been praying for him, and you."

"Wait. I'm a pity case?"

"Prayer isn't pity G. It is pure love. It takes time and effort. No one prays out of pity." He allowed that to sink in. "A lot of people … people who don't even know you … love you and your dad."

"How is that possible?"

"You're not so unlovable. Besides, nothing is impossible when there is love."

"I don't feel very lovable." She twirled her hair and took a sip of coffee. "How's it work, exactly?"

"What?

"Prayer. How do you know God is listening?"

"Oh." Nick took a seat at an empty table. Grey followed. "He's always listening."

"Well. I used to talk to Him a lot. I couldn't tell."

"What did you talk about?"

"Mainly, I just wanted to know why."

"Why?"

"Yeah. Why did He take my mom and dad?"

"Oh. That's a tough one." Nick rubbed his chin. "Grey, maybe you were asking the wrong question."

"Maybe."

"Maybe you should pray for peace."

"World peace?"

"You could start with peace in *your* world."

"That would be nice."

"Romans 8. Verses 26 and 28."

"Is that a prayer?"

"No. They are the two verses that just came to mind. Verse 26 says when you don't know what to pray for, the Holy Spirit will pray for you."

"That's handy. And verse 28?"

"God causes everything to work together for the good of those who love Him."

"I'm not sure I see the good."

"Some things take time, Grey. From my perspective, your circumstances brought you here. So far, that's a good thing."

"Yeah. So far, so good."

"Big picture, Grey, prayer is a conversation with God. It's you talking while He listens. And it's you listening for His answer. And when you are talking, it's not always a request. It can be praise or thanksgiving, a song or a poem, or sitting in silence and listening and letting the Holy Spirit guide the conversation.

"Thanksgiving?"

"You might not see it just now, but you have much to be thankful for. You have your health. You have Ray. Above all, you have a God who loves you and wants to connect with you.

"Wow. Seems like I've had this conversation."

"And?"

"Not sure I'm ready."

"It's okay. I'm praying for you." He winked. "Let's get back to work."

The days that followed were a lot like the first day. They started early, there was a rush of people, and then, suddenly, they were gone, and there was a lull. Then, it would start over. Grey got into the rhythm. She started getting her smile back. She was getting used to people asking about her and Ray. At first, she knew them by what they ordered – there was the double shot with cream, the skinny latte, the two tall Americano's to go – then, she started to catch their names and they started to call her "G" because they heard Nick call her that.

"Who's that gentleman in the back?" She asked.

"Which gentleman?"

"The one with the tweed jacket. He comes in every Tuesday, orders a small black coffee, and sits at that table. He's always meeting with someone different. Today, it looks like a line of people is waiting for him. Look."

"Oh, that's pastor Tom from the Lighthouse."

"Pastor Tom? Is this part of his church?" She chuckled.

"No, it's more like his office ... one day a week."

"Interesting."

Grey watched as the pastor greeted his visitors one after another. Everyone seemed to know that his table was private, and they gave him space to focus on the one person in front of him.

"Must be a pretty funky church," Grey mumbled.

"What do you mean?"

"All these people are so different. They don't look like they belong together. You know."

"Oh, that." Nick finished making a change for a customer. "Most of those people don't belong to his church. They just came here to see Tom. They ask for prayer or guidance or whatever is on their minds. You're right about the other thing, too."

"What other thing?"

"It is a funky church. Nearly closed its doors last year."

"I didn't know a church could go out of business."

"They can, and they do. This one is fighting back."

"Fighting? Against what? Hey. Who is that girl he is talking with? I've seen her before."

"What girl? Oh. Not sure. I think she's a poet or something."

"She's crying."

"Yeah. He gets a lot of that." Nick tapped her on the shoulder. "Look, we can talk about Tom and his church later. Right now, let's make some coffee."

"Sure. Sorry."

It was apparent Kendra had been crying, but she was oblivious to the rest of the people in the room. She needed to see the pastor. She mustered a smile as she took a seat.

"What's your name, dear?"

"Kendra," she said, wiping her eyes.

"I'm Tom, Kendra. What's troubling you?"

"Everything. Nothing. My life …" The dam broke, and the tears started to flow again. She tried to speak, but the words were stuck in her throat.

"It's okay, Kendra. Take your time." Pastor Tom had a way about him that made it easy for people to share. There was trust in his eyes as he peered into their life. Kendra caught her breath. She felt a calm come over her.

No, it came from within her. *How's that possible?* she thought. The pastor touched her hand.

"Let's start from the beginning."

Kendra talked about her life, her husband, and her dreams. She was writing her first novel, and while her husband supported her dream, finances were tight, and stress was high. They were new to town. And …

"Maybe you need to take a breath, Kendra."

"Okay."

"Really. Take a deep breath. In and out." She did. "Feels good, doesn't it?"

"It does. But …"

"No buts," he smiled. "It feels good. Enjoy the moment. Life is but a million little moments. You have to enjoy each one. Jesus said not to worry about tomorrow. Today brings enough worries of its own. So, enjoy the moment."

Kendra sat quietly. Breathing in and out.

Tom broke the silence. "Can you and your husband meet me this evening when he gets off work?"

"I think so," Kendra said cautiously.

"Good. That's when we'll start."

"Start what?"

"Do you love your husband?"

"Of course."

"And writing? Do you love your work?"

"I do."

"And life? Do you love life?"

"Most of the time."

"This evening, we will start working on loving life ALL the time," pastor Tom smiled a smile that went through Kendra and bounced around inside her head.

She smiled back.

"See you then."

"Thank you, Pastor."

"Thank you, Kendra."

He heals the brokenhearted and bandages their wounds.

Psalms 147:3 (NLT)

Chapter Five

It took a second surgery, physical therapy, and a lot of hard work before Ray got his hands back. It was nearly 18 months after the first surgery when he picked up a wrench and opened the hood of a car. The day he reopened, three customers dropped off their vehicles. Within a couple of weeks, it was like he had never closed. "The power of prayer," he liked to say. Grey wasn't so sure.

"I think you're just too stubborn to give up," she teased as she finished loading the dishwasher.

"Maybe so. Maybe so." He looked out the window. "But I hate to think where I would be without prayer."

On the seventh anniversary of the 'crash,' she said, "Hey, um, when I get off tomorrow afternoon, I'm taking flowers to Mom's gravesite. Do you … wanna go?"

"I would love to. You want me to come along?"

"Absolutely."

"Can you wait until four? I can close up then."

"Sure."

"So, you're not going to Alex's?"

"No. That was over the night of your surgery. That was the night that I stopped drinking and stopped hating. Besides, Alex left town. Barely said goodbye."

"That night was when I told you your mom was in Heaven."

"Wait a minute. You were serious? I thought it was just the drugs. What did you mean by that? How do you know?"

"G, she …" he took a breath. "Look, it's late. I'm beat. Can we talk about this tomorrow afternoon?"

"But." She stopped. She could see the look on his face. The look that said 'not tonight.' "Okay. Tomorrow afternoon at the cemetery. She'll be watching, so you better not try to back out."

Grey picked up some flowers the next day and was at the cemetery minutes later. She was mumbling to herself as she walked past the headstones and monuments. "I don't get it. I don't understand. God, help me understand." She arrived at her mom's site, and her mind flashed back to that day seven years ago when she watched as the earth swallowed her mom's casket. Just like that, she was gone. Just a memory. "But Ray says you are in Heaven now," she said out loud. She heard a twig snap behind her and turned to see Ray, also with flowers.

"Am I late?"

"No. I was talking to mom. Wondering what else I don't know about my own mother."

"Oh. About the 'Heaven' thing. It's no mystery, Grey. I talked to her that day before the crash."

"When she picked up her car?"

"No, as she was leaving the church."

"What? Why was she at church? That was a Wednesday afternoon."

"Walk with me." He took a big breath and slowly allowed the air to escape. "All I know is that she went to see Pastor Tom that day, and when she called me, she was ecstatic. She said she had recommitted her life to Jesus. She was happy, and there was a peace in her voice that I could feel through the phone. That's how I know she is in Heaven."

"I don't get it; we hadn't been to church in … years. Why? I just don't understand."

Ray and Grey found a bench and sat down. Ray relayed the conversations he and his wife had shared and the events that led to her visit to the church that day.

"Wait. You said she was talking to Pastor Tom?"

"Yes. At the Lighthouse Church downtown."

"I know him. Well, I don't know him exactly, but I see him when he comes to the coffee shop on Tuesdays.

"She might have met him there … probably did, now that I think about it. Don't you remember? He did the service seven years ago. Right over there."

"I guess I blocked that day from my memory. I don't know. I am so confused."

"It's okay, baby. Look, why don't you go see the pastor? He knows more than I do."

"I will," she said. "I mean. I probably will. I don't know if I'm ready."

"Ready for what?"

"Ready for church and all that stuff."

"By stuff, you mean religion?"

"Yeah. Stuff like that."

"Pastor Tom isn't like that. You'll see."

The Greatest Disciple in the World

Jesus said to the people who believed in him, "You are truly my disciples if you remain faithful to my teachings. And you will know the truth, and the truth will set you free."

John 8:32 (NLT)

Chapter Six

The next day, Grey thought about calling Pastor Tom. And the next day and the next. She thought about getting in line at the coffee shop on Tuesdays but didn't. Somehow, not knowing the answers to the questions she hadn't asked was better than asking the questions and getting the answers.

"Nick, do you ever wonder why sometimes it's better not to know than to know?"

"To not know what?" he quizzed.

"You know, stuff?"

"You *are* a mystery." He gazed out the window for a moment. "No. I think it's better to know than not know. In fact … I'm curious."

"About what?"

"You, Grey."

"I'm an open book."

"Right," he said wryly. "There's a few chapters unread."

"For instance?"

"Well, you've never mentioned a boyfriend or a date or …"

"Oh. That's easy. I don't date."

"Why's that?"

"Busy. Not interested. Most guys are …"

"Careful."

"Not ready for me and my mess."

"Oh. You don't seem that messy to me."

The Greatest Disciple in the World

"You don't want to know."

"You might be surprised."

"Oh, Nick. Look at the time. I have to run. I told Ray I would be home early. Can you close up?"

"Sure. But…"

"You're the best. See you."

"No. You're the best," he whispered as the door closed. "I don't think you know how good you are." Nick glanced at the mirror. "Well. What are you looking at? Oh, Lord, give me strength. I'm talking to myself." He locked the door and grabbed a broom.

Grey was early for work the following day, or so she thought. Nick's car was already there, but the "OPEN" sign wasn't lit, and he had posted a paper sign on the front door. "Closed today. See you tomorrow."

The only light in the room came from a couple of candles on the table where Nick was sitting.

"Why are we closed?" Grey asked as she took off her coat.

"I need to talk with you."

"Sounds serious."

"Yeah. You could kinda say that."

"Okay. What's up?"

"Coffee?"

"Of course." She studied his face. "Nick, what's on your mind?"

"This will probably come as a surprise to you. I know it was to me."

"Okay…."

"I. Uh. Grey. I'm in love."

"Great. Who's the lucky girl?"

"That's the thing." His eyes darted around the room like he was searching for something. He took a deep breath and closed his eyes for a moment. When he opened them, they were clear, calm, deep blue, staring into Grey. "It's you, Grey. I'm in love with you. I want to spend the rest of my life with you."

"You what? Are you nuts?" She jumped to her feet. The chair flew across the room.

"Probably."

"… seriously. You know how messed up I am. I was. I *still* am. You can't want to marry me."

Nick laughed. "You're right. I know that it doesn't make any sense, but I knew it the first day you walked in here. I couldn't *not* tell you." He looked down at the floor for a moment. "Hey, I know this is a shock. We haven't even 'dated' or gone out or talked about life or…"

"ANYTHING," she said.

"Right. Anything." He took a breath. "Look, I had to tell you. And I closed the shop today because I suspected we would need time to talk."

"You suspected right. Nick, I think you are a great guy —a great boss. But I am NOT going to marry you. Not now. Not ever."

"Take some time to think about it. We can start slow. I'm in no hurry. We can…"

"I don't need to think about it. In fact, I'm not sure I can work here anymore. I've got…I've got to get some air. I've gotta go."

"But…" before he could utter another syllable, she was gone.

Grey slammed her car door and drove away. Three blocks from the coffee shop, she pulled over, punched the steering wheel until her hands were numb, and screamed at the top of her lungs. "What just happened?" She looked into the rearview mirror, and she answered the question, "Well, you just lost your only friend and your job, and you just told the nicest guy in the world that you would never marry him. That's what happened, dummy." She sat in silence for a small eternity. "I think I'm gonna be sick."

Grey drove around for a couple of hours, trying to regain her composure. She pulled over again and grabbed her phone. "Maybe I can…dead? How can the battery be dead? Can this day get any worse?" She put the phone down and looked out the window. She had parked in front of the Lighthouse Church. The sign out front read "Answers Within." It was Pastor Tom's church. "Ha! I guess that's a sign," she laughed. She got out of the car and started toward the office. "No way he's here," she mumbled.

Be the Light

The Greatest Disciple in the World

Give all your worries and cares to God, for he cares about you.

1 Peter 5:7 (NLT)

Chapter Seven

Grey could hear the sound of music coming down the hall as she entered the church. She passed a room where someone was playing piano. She followed the hall to an open door. When she peaked inside, Pastor Tom was reading at his desk and making notes.

Tom looked up as she was about to knock. "Hi, Grey. What brings you here?"

Tom's office was bright, cheery, and smelled of leather and old books. Two walls were literally covered with books. Books on philosophy, history, art, and religion.

Tom's greeting took her by surprise. "You know me?"

"Of course. Every Tuesday at the coffee shop. Plus, I knew your mother."

"Right. Of course. I'm a little off today. Sorry."

"No problem. Come on in. Have a seat. How can I help you?"

"Pastor, I …"

"Please call me Tom."

"Pastor Tom."

"Or that."

"I. I am some kind of messed up. I don't even know where to start."

"Is this about your mom?"

"Well, not today. We'll get to that later. First, it's about Nick. He says, and I can't believe it. He says he wants to marry me!"

"It's about time."

"What do you mean? How do you know…?"

"Anyone can see by the way he looks at you. The way he is whenever you are around." He sat silently for a moment. "I take it you never noticed."

"No. Was it really that obvious?"

"I think smitten is the word. Yeah, 'smitten'. He's smitten with you."

"Apparently," she said.

"Is that a problem?" Tom asked.

"I guess marriage, or a 'relationship' of any type, was not on my radar," she sighed. "He caught me by surprise this morning."

"How so?"

"He closed the shop so he could propose."

"Wow. Pretty bold. Maybe you just need some time to process the idea," Tom offered.

"Yeah. I guess. But … I'm such a train wreck. I mean. I don't even know what 'love' is," she said with air quotes. "Why would anybody want to marry me? Look at this. Our marriage is on the rocks, and we haven't even set sail!"

"Hmmm. I see your point. Those are big questions." He was about to reach for a book. Instead, he paused for a full minute before he broke the silence. "Was there something else on your mind?"

"Well, I've been thinking about coming to see you for some time now."

"This is about your mother?"

"Yes, sir. Uh, Tom."

Tom leaned back in his chair. It was leather, well worn, and it breathed as he settled into it. She imagined he had leaned back like that thousands of times, thinking of what to say next.

He spoke first. "She was here the day of the accident. I guess you know that."

"I do now. I don't know why, and I had no idea she wanted to start attending church again. And, I ..."

"And you're still mad at God for taking her from you."

"Well. Yes. Yes, I am. I don't get it."

"Your mother was a great disciple, Grey."

"A disciple? What do you mean?"

"It wasn't that long ago that your mother sat in that very chair. She, too, was mad at God for taking your father. She had a lot of questions. She needed to unload a lot of what someone would call emotional baggage."

"And she did that here?"

"Some," he said. "But she worked out a lot of it on her own."

"So, why did you call her a disciple? We didn't go to church. She didn't preach on street corners. She didn't talk about God. At least not that I remember."

"Disciples ask questions, Grey. They are students. They know something is missing in their lives and want to learn and understand. That's how it begins." He looked out the window for a moment. "Do you believe in Jesus, Grey?"

"Yes. I think so. I mean, we used to go to church. I haven't thought about it for a long time. Maybe more lately. Working at Barnabas and all..."

"The original disciples had a lot of questions, too. They didn't understand a lot of what Jesus told them. They followed him, literally, and they listened and learned. Little by little, they came to understand. Even for them, though, it took Jesus' death and resurrection for it to all come together."

"Resurrection. Yeah, if my mother walked through that door right now, I think it would all come together for me, too."

Tom chuckled. "I get it. So, is that what you want? To understand? You want to be a disciple?"

"No, no, no. I'm no disciple. You don't know what kind of sinner I am. I'm not disciple material."

"That's funny."

"What do you mean? How is that funny?"

"That's what Simon, the fisherman, told Jesus. He was too much a sinner to be a disciple."

"What happened next?"

"Jesus said, 'Follow me, and I will make you a fisher of men,' and he became one of the greatest disciples in history."

"Great disciple? That's definitely not me."

"You have questions?"

"Yes."

"Would you like to know God better?"

"Maybe. I think so."

"You want to learn? To understand?"

"Yes. There's so much I don't understand."

"The first step in becoming a disciple is the willingness to learn and grow."

"I don't know."

"Grey, are you at peace?"

"Peace? No, I would say I'm not exactly at 'peace' yet."

"Would you like the peace of God?"

"Sure. Who wouldn't?"

"If you want the peace of God, you first have to be *at peace with* God."

"Well, you've got your work cut out for you."

"Yes, we do."

Tom let that sink in for a moment. Grey peered out the window. A tear glistened on her cheek.

"Grey, your mother told me she wasn't disciple material eight years ago. She felt the same as you. Think of it this way. A disciple starts as a student." Tom paused and added, "I think it really begins with a *desire* to learn. A desire to connect with a God, a higher power."

"Are there classes? Is there a test?"

"It's not like school, Grey. There's no graduation, per se. The test is life. The textbook is the Bible. As far as classes go, we will talk about it."

"Talk about it?"

"As I said, your mother figured out most things on her own. She would read the Bible, then come by, and we would talk. She asked questions. I introduced her to people who helped answer them."

"So that's it. I say yes, and I'm a disciple?"

"That's the beginning. You keep asking questions. You learn. You grow …"

"All right. What the h…? Oh. I'm sorry, pastor. I, uh…"

Tom laughed again. "You are so much like your mother … and a lot like Simon, I think." He stood up and came around his desk. As Grey started to rise, he said, "It's funny that you said you would believe if you saw your mother walk through that door."

"How's that?"

"Well. When I looked up about twenty minutes ago, I could have sworn she did. You are so much like her."

Tears formed in Grey's eyes. "I don't know what to say," she mumbled.

"Just say you'll come back." He picked up a Bible from his desk. "Here, this is for you. I gave your mother one just like it."

Grey took the book and turned to leave. She stopped, turned around, and hugged Tom. "I don't think I know what happened here or what is next, but … Thank you," she said. "Thank you."

That night, Grey sat in silence while Ray watched TV.

"Are you okay?" He asked.

"Sure."

"So, not really?"

"I'm sorry. I'm not myself."

"Who are you?"

"Good question."

"Seriously. What's going on?"

"How did you know?"

"Know what?"

"How did you know that mom was the one?"

"Oh. That's easy. She came into the shop one day in an old clunker with 250,000 miles on it. I knew immediately."
"What?"
"I knew she was going nowhere without my help."
"Come on. I'm serious."
"Grey, from the moment I saw her. The moment she spoke to me. I knew she was the one."
"Yeah. That's what Nick said."
"He finally spoke up?"
"You could say so. He…" She paused.
"He what?"
"He proposed."
"Whoa. How did that go over?"
"Like you would expect."
"Ouch."
"He closed the shop today, and when I walked in, he told me he was in love. In love with ME."
"Well, it's about time."
"You, too?"
"Well. Yes. It was all over his face. I think it's all over town."
"I guess I never noticed," she winced. "I just. I don't know. So, really, how did you know?"
"Grey. Love isn't fireworks or a sudden flash of light. I mean, it can start that way, but not always."
"So, how do you know?"
"Love is finding the person that you 'want' to love."
"That makes no sense."
"Sure it does."

The Greatest Disciple in the World

"How?"

"When I met your mom, I saw a beautiful person. Beautiful on the outside but, most importantly, beautiful on the inside."

"What does that mean?"

"She made me feel special from the moment we met. Me, a grubby mechanic with grease-stained hands and a high school diploma."

"Nothing wrong with that."

"That's what she said. Not with words but with actions and her smile," he hesitantly said. "I looked at her, and I could see the future. As I got to know her, I wanted to know more. I wanted to be with her and do everything I could to make her life better. I wanted the best for her."

"And?"

"And that meant whatever was best. Even if that didn't include me."

"What?"

"Grey. Love is not a feeling. Love is more about something you want to do. It's a verb. An action. I knew that I wanted to love your mother … to want the best for her … no matter what."

"No matter what?" Grey started to get up. "Did she feel the same?"

"Not at first. In the beginning, she was just the nicest person I'd ever met." Ray laughed. "I guess I kind of grew on her. So, how do you feel about Nick?"

"I don't know. I mean. I hadn't thought about him that way until today. I did learn today that I think he's one of the nicest ... if not THE nicest ... guys in the world. That caught me by surprise."

"In the world?"

"Well, he is. He's super thoughtful. He's kind and generous. You should see how he cares about people he doesn't even know ..."

"Oh, I've seen..."

"He gives away almost as much coffee as he sells. He helps struggling artists."

"I know Grey, I ..."

"I do like spending time with him. He's not really a boss. He's more of a ..."

"Friend? Maybe a good friend?"

"Yes. A friend."

"Why don't you explore that friendship?" He asked. "See where it goes?"

Grey stood up and walked to the desk where she left her phone. "Okay. What the heck? He *is* the nicest guy I know. Next to you, of course."

"Of course."

The Greatest Disciple in the World

For we are God's masterpiece. He has created us anew in Christ Jesus so we can do the good things he planned for us long ago.

Ephesians 2:10 (NLT)

Chapter Eight

The next day, again, Grey was at work early. The lights were on this time, the door was unlocked, and Nick was busy making coffee. He paused as she took off her coat. "Grey, about yesterday, I'm sorry. I don't know what I was thinking."

"I think you were thinking that you love me and want to spend your life with me. Is that what you're sorry about?"

"No. Not that exactly ... I was just ..."

"Stop. Nick, I am the one who should apologize. I'm sorry I reacted the way I did." She reached for the cup of coffee Nick had poured for her. "I guess I should pay more attention. I had no idea. Apparently, I was the only one in town who didn't know?" The question hung in the air as she stared at Nick with a 'what the heck' look on her face. He laughed. She laughed.

"Well. I never told anyone, but you know how that worked out."

They laughed together as the door swung open, and the first customers eased in. "I guess we'll talk about this later, okay?"

"Sure."

It was a busy day at the Barnabas. Lots of questions about why the shop was closed the day before. "Is everything okay?" "Was someone sick?" "Do you need anything?" Grey was impressed that so many people truly cared. *It's not just coffee that brings them in*, she thought.

The Greatest Disciple in the World

As they were closing and cleaning up, Nick broke the ice. "How do you feel about dinner?"

"I like dinner," she smiled. "It's one of my three favorite meals."

"I mean, what do you say we go out sometime and have a meal? Get to know each other a little better?"

"You mean like a date?"

"Yes. But I know you said you don't date, and I've never seen you …"

"I think I'll make an exception for you."

"Saturday night, then?"

"Saturday night."

That evening, Grey was reading while Ray was paying bills at the kitchen table. Out of the blue, she asked, "Do you think I'm like Simon?"

"Who?" Ray scratched his head and smiled. "No, I would say you're more like Alvin. Definitely not Theodore. Not that you aren't smart." He stopped scratching and pointed up. "Definitely, Alvin."

"Not Simon the Chipmunk, you goof. Simon Peter, the disciple."

"Oh," Ray scratched his head again. "Is he the one who told Jesus he was wrong, denied him three times… the impetuous one, talks without thinking, always right, rarely listens? *That* Simon?"

"That's the one."

"No," he said with a twinkle in his eye. "You are not like Simon; he was a fisherman. You're not a fisherman."

"Funny."

Ray pondered for a moment. "So, you're reading the Bible?"

"Yeah, Pastor Tom gave it to me. He said the answers are all in here."

"To which questions?"

"I'm working on that. Between the parables and the Beatitudes, I'm thoroughly confused."

"Patience, Grey. Patience."

"Easy for you to say," she breathed. "Not exactly my strong suit," she said with a smile.

Ray went back to his paperwork. Grey went back to reading. "I wish I were a fisherman," she mumbled. "Fishing is bound to be easier."

A week later, she went back to the Lighthouse Church. Tom was meeting with one of the church committees. "Come on in, we were just finishing. Thanks, everyone. You all know Grey from the coffee shop, right?"

She exchanged pleasantries as they were leaving. She recognized several faces but knew only a few of the names. *Friendly group*, she thought. "The lady in the red sweater. Iced coffee."

"That's Regina." He wrinkled his nose. "Iced coffee?"

"Yeah. She comes to the shop just about every day, and she always gets an iced coffee. Summer or winter. Always iced coffee. I know people more by what they order than by their names," she explained. "You were 'small, black coffee.'"

"Of course."

Grey settled into the chair opposite Tom and reached into her backpack. "Pastor, I am so confused. I don't know where to start."

"Perfect," Tom replied.

"How is that perfect?"

"Well, if you had all the answers already, we wouldn't have much to talk about, would we?"

"I guess not. I mean, I see your point, but isn't it supposed to be easier?"

"What? Life? The Bible? Christianity?"

"Exactly. All of it. Why is it so difficult?"

"You want to understand, right? You want to know God?"

"I admit it. I am spiritually bankrupt, okay?"

"Grey, the Kingdom of Heaven is yours."

"There you go, Pastor, talking in riddles. That comes from the Sermon on the Mount. I've read it at least a dozen times. I don't get it. *'The meek will inherit the earth. The pure in heart will see God!'* Who is pure in heart? What does it mean?"

"Slow down. Slow down. You're on a journey, Grey. A long, slow journey. It's not a sprint. Not even a marathon. Just slow down and take it one step at a time. One small, baby step at a time."

Tom looked out the window. There was a robin perched on the branch of a large oak tree. It was so close that he could hear the tune the bird was singing. He listened for a minute or two. Grey let out a fake cough to regain his attention.

"Grey. Take a look at that robin." She glanced in the direction of the window. "Seriously. Look at that bird. Not a care in the world. It finds a mate. Builds a nest. Feeds its babies. Sings the day away. That's pretty much it. No worries."

"And …?"

"And God loves that bird. He gives it life and sunshine and worms to eat. He loves it."

"Okay."

"But he doesn't love that bird as much as He loves you."

"How's that?"

"God didn't send His son to earth to connect with the birds. He sent him so that He could have a relationship with you."

"Me?"

"Yes. You. And all of humanity. You are God's masterpiece, and He wants to spend time with you. He wants to see you grow and mature and …"

"Be all that I can be?"

"Yes. And be all that you can be." Tom paused while he studied the bird. "And the difference between you and that bird is that you were made to connect with God. You were made to know Him and for Him to know you. When you say you are spiritually bankrupt, you are saying something a bird cannot say… if it could talk. Instinctively, you know you were made for something more than mere existence. You are a daughter of the Creator of the Universe, and He wants you to get to know Him and His Son."

"Okay. I'm not sure about being a 'masterpiece,' but I'm ready. Ready as I'll ever be. Where do we start?"

"I think bankruptcy is a good place to begin. And, since you brought it up, I think we'll start with the Sermon on the Mount. Tomorrow, I'm going to introduce you to someone who was also spiritually bankrupt. She'll help show you the way."

"Introduce?"

"Actually, you already know her. Red sweater. Iced coffee."

"Iced coffee? Oh. Regina."

"Yes. I'll ask her to come by the coffee shop tomorrow at 3 pm. You get off at 3, right?"

"Yes. Tomorrow is good." She glanced at the robin. "Are you sure about the Sermon on the Mount? That's where I should start. Really?

"I'm sure. That sermon laid down the foundation for Christianity. It paved a path, a stairway, that connects us to God."

"A Stairway to Heaven, really?"

Tom laughed. "I hadn't thought about that song. Yes. A stairway, but you don't buy your way there. You don't earn it. It is a journey, Grey. Regina will get you started tomorrow."

"Okay. I'll take it one stair step at a time," she smiled.

"That's the spirit."

Be the Light

The Greatest Disciple in the World

Come close to God, and God will come close to you.
James 4:8 (NLT)

Chapter Nine

'Iced Coffee' Regina appeared right on time the next day. Grey greeted her with more than a bit of apprehension in her voice. She extended her hand. "Hi, I'm Grey. Happy to …"

Regina broke through the moment and wrapped Grey up in a hug as if they had been friends since childhood. "Oh, Grey, I am so excited. I have looked forward to this day for eons."

"I'm not even going to ask what that means," Grey said. "It seems my life is more of an open book than I could have imagined."

"Not to worry, Grey. I'm happy to share my story and hopefully help you on your journey. When Tom called, I told him I would be honored."

Grey motioned to a quiet table in the corner. "Regina, Pastor Tom gave me this Bible. He said the answers are here, but I have more questions than answers."

"I know exactly how you feel. I was there, too. I wanted to understand. To connect, but I felt empty. Spiritually, I was … I don't know, I was just…"

"Bankrupt?"

"That's it. Bankrupt. You, too?"

"Yes. And when I told the pastor, he said, 'The Kingdom of Heaven is yours.'"

"Ah, the Beatitudes."

"Yes. Those da– uh, dang Beatitudes."

Regina opened her satchel, pulled out her Bible, and laid it on the table. "I'll be right back. First, I need to see a man about …."

"An iced coffee?"

"Exactly."

"Nick has it ready for you. He's bringing it over now. My treat."

"How sweet! Thank you, Grey. And thank you, Nick."

She took a long sip of the icy brew. "Just what the doctor ordered," she gulped. "So, where do we start? The beginning, I guess."

"Genesis?" laughed Grey.

"This *is* going to be fun! No, let's start with the Sermon on the Mount and those dang Beatitudes."

"Aren't sermons supposed to make sense?" asked Grey. "Was Jesus trying to be obtuse? Was he speaking in code?"

"I know it does seem that way, but no, He was kicking off His ministry, introducing the Kingdom of Heaven, and explaining the path, the heart change, if you will, to become one of His followers. In other words, a disciple."

"Okay. First things first. What does it mean?"

"What does what mean?"

"Beatitude. It can't be English, can it?"

"Oh. I'm sorry. I guess we do sometimes speak in code."

"Is it a noun or a verb…or an adjective…or what?"

"I would call it a descriptive noun."

"Is that a real thing?"

"Technically?....maybe not. The Greek word for beatitude means happy or blessed, so a Beatitude is a blessing that describes a happy state."

Grey looked perplexed. "Okay. So 'blessed are the poor in spirit'... sounds like the sad are happy."

"I guess it does when you say it like that."

"And 'for theirs is the Kingdom of Heaven.' What the heck does that mean?"

"First, let me try a different perspective on the word Beatitude."

"I'm game."

"Jesus' sermon and the beatitudes describe the pathway to the faith that leads to the Kingdom of God."

"Okay."

"And the beatitudes are what your '*attitude should be*' to follow that path."

"So. This is about faith?" Regina nodded. "But, I thought faith was blind."

"I think God would rather you follow him with your eyes open."

"Okay. So, the Sermon and the Beatitudes are all about faith?"

"In simple terms, yes."

"That's not so complicated. But are the poor in spirit happy or sad?"

"That's an easy one, Grey," Regina smiled. "When you told Pastor Tom that you were spiritually bankrupt, you were saying you didn't feel God's Spirit or presence."

"That's right. It feels like God has abandoned me."

"You need to make room for Him."

"Come again?"

"You have to make room … mentally and spiritually … for Him."

"So, if I know I am spiritually bankrupt, I have to become 'poor in spirit' so …"

"Yes. That's why the pastor said…"

"The kingdom of Heaven is mine. Okay." Grey threw up her hands. "I'm sorry, I still don't get it."

"Poor in spirit doesn't mean sad or depressed or angry. It means you recognize that you *need* God and are less than whole without Him." She paused. "Grey, maybe you've heard that everyone has a 'God-sized' hole in their heart, and they will never feel complete until that hole is filled. There will always be something missing."

"I've heard something like that, I think."

"Poor in spirit means that *your spirit, your ego, your pride, your desire to be in control* is made less so you can make room for God's Spirit. It means that you admit you can't do it on your own and that you need God's help. It's the first step in discovering yourself and your purpose. It's the first step in opening the door to let God in."

"So why didn't Jesus just say that?"

"He did, Grey. Those who heard His sermon two thousand years ago knew exactly what He meant. But our language is different, and what was once clear is now, as you said, obtuse."

"Lost in translation," Grey whispered, peering into the words in her Bible.

Regina let this new perspective hang in the air while she sipped her coffee. She could see Grey was processing and about to ask a question.

"So, the first step in knowing God is admitting I need Him. And when I do that, I am making room. Becoming 'poor in spirit.' That's the 'key' to the Kingdom?"

"I hadn't thought about it that way, but yes. That's the key to the Kingdom." Grey smiled. Regina took another sip of her coffee. "So, Grey, to make room for God, you must shrink your ego and put yourself in the back seat."

"Back seat?"

"That's right. Grey. I've seen you here at the coffee shop. You seem pretty confident. Pretty together. You probably don't feel 'poor in spirit.' Am I right?"

"You should have seen me a few years ago. I was a big, hot mess," she hesitated. "I think deep inside, I still am a mess. I just put up a good front." Again, she paused. "And this whole 'disciple' thing has me a little unnerved."

"I understand." Regina took a deep breath. "Look. I used to be a self-reliant, make-my-own-way, take-no-prisoners kind of girl. Some called me arrogant. I called it confidence."

"You still seem pretty confident."

"I am. The difference is this. When my confidence comes from within or from my circumstances or my job, there will come a day when I will fail, my circumstances will change, or I will lose my job. At that moment, I will have nothing to hold onto. Nothing to support my ego, my pride."

"So 'poor in spirit' means humble?"

"That's part of it. The humble disciple knows she needs God's grace and His salvation. She needs His strength and support. She is repentant and asks God for forgiveness, guidance, and direction. She looks to Him for hope and peace, no matter the circumstances. It's also about trust."

"So, when things go wrong or bad or out of my control, I am okay because I know I am not in control. He is."

"There you go."

"And when I accept God into my heart, when I let him take the wheel, so to speak, the Kingdom of Heaven is mine? I will be blessed?"

"I think you're getting it."

"Maybe…"

"Think about it for a day or two. Let it sink in. Study the notes you've been taking." Regina started to get up.

"Wait. What about the next one? The next Beatitude?

"You've had enough for one day, Grey." She finished her coffee, stood up, and put a five-dollar bill on the table. "A tip for the excellent service," she winked.

"But…"

"Check in with Pastor Tom when you're ready. Take your time, Grey. This is important stuff."

"Thanks, Iced Coffee…I mean Regina." She blushed. "Sorry."

"No worries. I'll see you tomorrow," she winked. "When I come in for my iced coffee."

Be the Light

The Greatest Disciple in the World

Do not despise these small beginnings ...
Zechariah 4:10 (NLT)

Chapter Ten

That night, after supper, Grey was reading her notes, comparing notes with her Bible, and comparing different translations on her Bible app.

"There must be a dozen different ways to interpret the Beatitudes," she said out loud.

Ray looked up from his book. "Didn't think I would ever hear you say the word 'Beatitudes'," he chuckled. "Your mother asked me what I thought they meant. I told her it was Greek to me."

"I think that's the problem. It was Greek or something," she laughed. "Of course, it could be that you just need to empty your spirit."

"Right. I'll let you explain all that to me when you figure it out." He shook his head and went back to his book.

Undeterred, Grey went on. "Empty your spirit means poor in spirit, which means you're ready to give up or give in. It's when you realize that you aren't in control anymore. As if you ever were."

Ray looked up again. "And you start to pray."

The lightbulb started to flicker for Grey. "And when you ask God for help, you bring Him in; you take the first step toward the Kingdom of God, and … you are blessed."

Ray countered, "So, what if He doesn't answer your prayer?"

"Beats me."

"Well, since He *is* in control, I guess no answer is an answer. Or maybe He is just saying *not right now*."

"Maybe." Grey grinned, "You know you're pretty smart for an old guy who never went to college."

"Layers, baby, layers. Just like Shrek. I'm an onion."

"Guess that's why Mom thought you hung the moon."

"Yeah. Enough about me," he said as he got up from his chair. "Grey. I'm sure Tom must have told you this is a journey, and you have to take it one step at a time. If you try to drink from a fire hose, you will spill a lot of water. Just take a sip at a time, and let each sip sink in."

"Right. Patience is my middle name."

Ray gave her a pat on the shoulder. "Don't worry, Abigail, you'll get it. Oops. I mean Grey."

"It's okay, Dad. It's okay."

Be the Light

If you try to hang on to your life, you will lose it. But if you give up your life for my sake and for the sake of the Good News, you will save it.

Mark 8:35 (NLT)

Chapter Eleven

Two days later, Grey called Tom. When she walked into his office, she fell into the chair in front of his desk. "The Kingdom of Heaven," she exclaimed.

"Good afternoon, Grey."

"Sorry, Pastor. I've got a new question. I'm searching for the Kingdom of Heaven or the Kingdom of God or whatever it is."

"Good," he said.

"Not good," she replied. "I don't get it. I mean…it's Heaven, right?"

"It is…"

"I'm not ready for Heaven."

"…and it's not."

Grey stared at Tom with one of those 'what the heck is that supposed to mean?" looks on her face. Tom got up and walked around to the chair beside Grey.

"Jesus said, '…the Kingdom of God is within you.' (KJV) In some translations, he says, '…the Kingdom of God is already among you.' (NLT) So, Grey, it *is* about Heaven, but it is also about the here and now. It's about you."

"How is that?"

"It's about you, the disciple. As you learn and grow and begin to understand and experience the blessings, the joy, the peace, and the hope that comes from a deep relationship with God, you will understand that the Kingdom of God is here and now, and it's within you. Jesus said 'The Kingdom of God is at hand.' If you accept that, Grey, you will stop fighting with God and start working with him."

Grey let out a sigh. "I'm fighting with God? Regina said that, too."

"Sure, everybody does. We fight to be in control. We fight to resist His plan for us. We fight against the commandments. We worship people or products or our own pride. We desperately want to be in charge. Self-reliant. Independent."

"I can see that."

"And it's very lonely."

"I definitely can see that." Grey picked up her notebook and thumbed through the pages. "Regina explained that the poor in spirit means the ones who have emptied themselves *of themselves*…" She paused and looked up at Tom.

"Think of it like this, Grey. You are a vessel, a container like a bottle or a glass. If your glass is full of yourself, your idols, your fears, and your plans, there's no room for God. So, like a glass, you must empty it before refilling it. You have to empty yourself of your *'self.'* Once you do that and invite God in, you will begin to discover the Kingdom of God within. You'll soon realize that your glass is no longer a 12-ounce glass. It's an ocean with endless possibilities. When you let God in, you have lots of room for other 'priorities,'" he said with air quotes.

"I was talking with Ray the other night. We figure it starts with prayer."

"Prayer is God's favorite channel," he smiled. "Better than anything on social media or TV."

"No subscription, either. So, what do I do next?"

"Next and always, you trust God. Remember, this is about faith."

"And I'll live happily ever after, right?"

Pastor Tom laughed. "Good question. No, Grey. Troubles will still come your way: hardships and unexpected problems. The Christian life is not automatically easier. In some ways, it can be more challenging, but things have a way of working out how they are supposed to, and that's usually for good. We'll get more into that later. For now, let's proceed with the Beatitudes and keep you moving on your journey. I've asked another friend to help with the next lesson. I think you'll like him. His name is Alex.

Your love for one another, will prove to the world that you are my disciples.

John 13:35 (NLT)

Chapter Twelve

"You cut your hair!" Grey exclaimed as Alex walked into the Coffee shop. "And you never said goodbye or that you were back. Where've you been?"

"Slow down. Slow down."

Grey walked up to Alex as if to hug him. Instead, she punched him in the shoulder. "There," she said. Shaking her hand. "Dang Alex. That wasn't supposed to hurt *me.*"

Alex laughed. "Good to see you, too. And thanks for calling me Alex and not…"

"Turkey?"

"Right."

"I'm trying to do better."

"Good. Me, too."

"Where have you been, and what will you teach me about the Bible? And since when are you qualified to … you know … "

"Wow. You are full of questions." Alex sat down and set his Bible on the table. "Well, I'm still learning, too, but I guess Pastor Tom thought I could help since I just graduated from Seminary, and …"

"Wait. What?"

"And that answers the part about where I've been."

"So, you are a preacher now? A pastor? A reverend?"

"Uh, sure. I start next month at my new church."

"Whoa. I think I better sit down." She eased into a chair and took a sip from her coffee. "How? When? I had no idea."

"The short answer is: I'm a disciple, just like you. Years ago, I went to Tom with questions. One thing led to another, and here we are."

"I had no idea."

"Me neither. God's plans aren't always obvious until …" Alex scratched his head. "Well, they aren't obvious until they are."

"Obviously," G added.

They laughed.

"You guys need anything?" It was Nick. Grey jumped up.

"Nick. This is Alex. My old friend from my darker days," she said.

"Hi, Alex. I am so glad to meet you. I have heard a lot about you. You were a good friend to my girl."

Alex got up to shake Nick's hand. "I tried."

"Nick is my boss," Grey interjected. "And … we're kind of dating."

"Wow. You said you would never."

"It was kind of a compromise," Nick said. "After she turned down my marriage proposal."

"Can we talk about something else?" Grey asked.

All three burst into laughter. Nick sat down with them, and they talked briefly about Alex's travels, his plans, and how Pastor Tom had asked him to help Grey in her studies.

The bell jingled as a new customer entered the front door. "I guess that's my cue to get back to work. If you two need anything, give me a shout."

"Will do," said Alex.

"Thanks, Nick." G pulled out her notebook. "This is going to be interesting."

"So, where would you like to start?"

"Well, Pastor Tom said I need to understand the Beatitudes. I'm not sure that is possible."

Alex sat back in his chair. "Go ahead," he urged.

"'Blessed are those who mourn, for they will be comforted.' Well, that can't be true. I mourned my mother for years and never felt comforted or blessed. And 'blessed are the meek,' Nobody has ever called me 'meek,' so I would say I'm pretty much screwed on that one, too."

Alex was quiet for a moment or two. For Grey, it seemed an eternity. "Grey, let's look at these statements differently. They make no sense when you try to apply or understand them literally in modern-day terms. Think of the Beatitudes, these blessings, as a set of stairs leading to a relationship *with God and for God.*"

"Right. The stairway to Heaven. The first step is poor in spirit."

"That's right. Before you can approach God, you have to make room for Him, His Spirit. You have to give up yourself. You know that part."

"I understand. Pastor Tom and Regina explained it. Even Ray helped."

"Great. And how did that make you feel?"

"Well, a little sad. And lonely."

"Did you mourn your loss?"

"Did I mourn..." and her eyes went wide. "You are kidding me. That's what it means? To be 'sad' that I am alone..."

"That's part of it, Grey," he added, "but let's discuss why you are alone. Pastor Tom said you thought you were too much of a sinner to be a disciple."

"Just like Simon Peter," she laughed.

"Think about who your friends were a few years ago."

"Friends? Except for you, I didn't have any."

"Not so, Grey. You were very close friends with Anger, Resentment, Self-Pity, even Hate."

"Oh. Those friends."

"Yes. And as long as they were part of your life, there was little room for anything else."

"You're right. I was a total…"

"But when you started to embrace Forgiveness, Peace, and Love, what happened?"

Grey thought for a long moment. "Well, to start with, I felt like a jerk for acting the way I did, especially to Ray."

"And did that make you sad? Did you mourn your behavior?"

"I did," she smiled. "I didn't think about it, but that's exactly what happened. I was embarrassed and sad that I had been so stupid."

"So, when Jesus said 'blessed are those who mourn,' he was talking about you."

"Okay."

"And when you lament your sins and reject those old friends of anger and hate, you realize just how far you are from God and how much you need his grace and peace in your life."

"So, when I mourn my 'sin' and how it has separated me from God and then reject my past behavior, I am blessed with God's presence?"

"I've heard it said that you must first realize you are powerless before you can be powerful. Likewise, you must admit that you are foolish before becoming wise."

"I must admit I am weak before I can become strong?"

"Yes. We mourn our failures … the things that distance us from God … before we can be blessed."

"Wow." Grey stood up and stretched, pacing and mumbling. Alex went to get a cup of coffee. When he came back, she was ready.

"So, what about meek? You know I'm kind of like the opposite …"

"You are strong, Grey, at least on the outside. But we can't go to God in strength. You go to God *for* strength. When you approach God modestly, without arrogance, and free from pride, He will fill you with a strength that is beyond comprehension." Alex took a moment to stop and look up. Grey's face was twisted into a question.

"And when I am meek, I will inherit the earth?"

"In a manner of speaking, yes. You will be a child of God, the creator of the earth and everything in it. But let's focus on the first part. A child of God."

"And if I am God's child?"

"He will teach and guide you. Just as you will teach your children someday."

"Stay focused, Alex. I'm a long way from having children to teach."

"I heard that!" Nick chuckled from behind the counter.

"Right," Alex said shyly. "This takes us to the next step on the stairway: 'Blessed are those who hunger and thirst for righteousness, for they will be filled. They will be satisfied."

"Righteousness? What the …"

"Righteousness. I know it sounds a little churchy…"

"Like Ray says, it's Greek to me," she smiled.

"Grey, if you want 'righteousness', it means you simply want to live 'right' and have a right relationship with God. It means you want to do His will."

"His will?"

"Do you remember the great commandments?"

"The 10?"

"No. The two. Jesus was asked which commandment was the most important. His answer was two commandments. Love God with all your heart, mind, and soul, and equally important —love people."

"That's right. I read that. Two is easier than ten."

"That's God's will. If you love and honor God, you will do what's right."

"Thy will be done," she smiled. "That's part of the Lord's Prayer."

"Correct, when the disciples asked Jesus to teach them to pray, he taught them what we now call the Lord's Prayer." Alex opened his Bible.

"It's here in the book of Matthew. Thy Kingdom come, thy will be done on earth as it is in Heaven."

"The Kingdom of God is at hand."

"Yes, Grey. If you want to know God and have more peace and joy in your life … no matter what happens …

He's ready. The door is open. His Kingdom is at hand. On earth as in Heaven."

"Okay. I walk through the door. You said He will teach me. How does He teach me?"

"Right here," Alex answered as he held up his Bible. "And right here," he pointed to himself. "And all around you, if you are paying attention."

"Okay. So, if I recognize my need for God and express sorrow that He is not currently present in my life while humbly seeking to understand Him, I can walk through His door and be a disciple?"

Alex took a deep breath. "You always did know how to get straight to the point." He smiled. "You are making great progress, kid. You're getting it much faster than I did."

"Must be I have better teachers," Grey grinned.

Alex stood to go. "I think you should reflect on what we've talked about. I'll be in town for another week or so if you want to talk more."

"Always sending me home before I'm ready to go," she said as she hugged him. "Is it okay to hug a 'Reverend'?"

"Absolutely. My boss doesn't mind if yours doesn't."

Grey drew back as if to hit him again and, remembering the pain of the first hit, thought better of it. "Thanks, Alex. You always were a good friend."

"Your best friend," he smiled.

"Best and only," she replied.

The Greatest Disciple in the World

Jesus called out to them, "Come, follow me, and I will show you how to fish for people!"
                                   Matthew 4:19 (NLT)

Chapter Thirteen

Grey decided to go for a walk to consider all she had learned. Before she realized it, she was back at The Lighthouse. "It's like deja vu all over again," she chuckled. Children were playing on the church playground. She sat in a swing and watched the kids climb the jungle gym and spin around on the merry-go-round. Without thinking, she closed her eyes, took a deep breath, and prayed. "God, I am a mess. But of course, you know that. I want your will to be done with *me*. I don't know why you would care, but it seems you have placed people in my life that…"

"Who are you talking to?"

Grey opened her eyes. The voice came from the wide-eyed, quizzical face of a young girl suddenly standing before her.

"I'm Mandy," the little face said. "I'm eight."

"Hi, Mandy. I'm G. I mean Grey. People call me Grey. I, uh, I was talking to God."

"Why?"

"Well, He's my Father, and I'm supposed to go to Him when I have questions."

"I don't have a father."

"I'm sorry."

"It's okay. I talk to my Mom."

"Oh," Grey paused. "Yeah, I don't have a Mom."

"Too bad. Mom's are fun," Mandy threw over her shoulder as she bounded back toward the merry-go-round.

"No kidding," Grey winced.

"Making new friends?" Grey looked around. It was Pastor Tom.

"I guess."

"How was your lesson with Alex?"

"You didn't tell me he had gone to seminary."

"Life is full of surprises, isn't it?"

"I'll say." Grey hesitated for a moment. "I started praying a minute ago."

"Good."

"Well, maybe. It's just … I didn't know what to say."

"Grey, you took the first step. Don't worry. The words will come. Sometimes, you just need to listen."

"Listen? To what?"

"Listen to your thoughts. Open your Bible. Open your heart. Just listen."

"My thoughts," she pondered. "Do you think He wants to know what I'm thinking?"

Tom laughed. "He knows what you're thinking. He knows your questions, your fears, your hopes and dreams…"

"Does He know I'm still mad about Mom?"

Tom went silent. "Yes. Grey. He knows." He looked into the distance for a minute. Slowly, he turned back to Grey. There was a hint of a tear in his eye. "But He needs to hear it from you. I can't explain it, but I can tell you without question the only way a prayer gets answered is after it is asked."

"What if I don't like the answer?"

"Well. At least you'll have an answer."

"Oh. I guess you're right," she muttered. "So, how do I start?"

"Find a quiet place. On a swing, in your car, in your bedroom, at the coffee shop. Any quiet place will work. Any quiet time will work. King David was alone in a cave when he wrote many of the Psalms. Often, he started angry and upset. He felt alone and abandoned. Ultimately, though, he trusted God and found his way out of the cave."

"So, it's okay if I yell at Him a little bit?"

"Better out than in."

"You're quoting Shrek, now?"

"Hmmm. Guess so."

They laughed. And it felt good.

"Thank you, pastor."

"I'll leave you alone now. Remember, He is ready whenever you are."

The Greatest Disciple in the World

There are different kinds of gifts, but the same Spirit distributes them. There are different kinds of service, but the same Lord.

1 Corinthians 12:4-5 (NIV)

Chapter Fourteen

The next day at the Barnabas Coffee Shop was a busy one. Nick and Grey were non-stop until after two. When there was a lull in the storm, Grey took a deep breath, poured two cups of coffee, and sat at a two-top near the front. Nick followed with a couple of cookies.

"Lunch," he said as he plopped into the seat.

"Thanks."

"It might be time to hire some help," he said as he bit into the cookie.

"I second that idea."

They sat in silence while the radio played in the background.

"What does that mean? Grey asked, pointing in the direction of the music. "Stop holding on and just be held."

Nick listened to the song and thought for a moment. "You know how we want to be in charge? We want to control our environment and our emotions. We want things to be the way we want them to be?"

"Are you calling me a 'control freak'?"

"Ha!" Nick couldn't contain his laughter. "You're kidding, right?"

Grey just stared at him until she could no longer hold it in. She burst into laughter, too.

"Okay. I admit it. What's your point?"

"We all want control. It's natural."

"And?"

"Fact is, we have no control, Grey. None. When something funny happens, we laugh. When something sad happens, we cry. When something good happens, we're happy."

"And when something bad happens, we're angry."

"So, stop holding on to the idea that you are in control. Let go and let God hold your troubles, problems, and fears. Just be held."

"That's what Pastor Tom said."

"You know he's usually right."

"Usually?"

"Ha! That's my girl."

Their laughter was interrupted by the tinkle of the bell as it announced the arrival of another customer.

Nick jumped to his feet. "I'll take care of this order. You just relax. Just be held." He winked as he slid behind the counter.

Grey sipped her coffee and nibbled at the oatmeal cookie in her hand. She was staring out the window. A bird was circling overhead. "So, little birdie. What's next?" Without thinking, she said, "Okay, God. I give up. I'm a mess, but now I'm *your* mess."

She opened her Bible, the one Tom had given her. Inside the cover was an inscription she had never seen before. It read, *In life, the only thing that you can control is how you react to God and His promise. - Tom*

"Well. I guess that takes care of that." She smiled and closed the book.

Be the Light

The Greatest Disciple in the World

A new command I give you: Love one another. As I have loved you, so you must love one another.
John 13:34 (NIV)

Chapter Fifteen

Grey's next lesson took her to a neighborhood on the outskirts of town. A cottage-style house with a white fence and a Thank You Jesus sign in the front yard. She saw a familiar face when the door opened.

"Kendra! I didn't know I would be seeing you today."

"Welcome to my humble abode, Grey. Come on in. Take a seat. Would you like a cup of coffee?"

"Sure."

"Great. I'll serve you for a change."

"Kendra, I haven't seen you at the coffee shop lately."

"Yeah. I've been working to finish a big project. The deadline is coming fast, so I've been hunkered down here at the house."

"Oh. Are you sure you have time for this?"

"Absolutely. I can use a break. How do you like your coffee?"

"Black is perfect. Thanks."

Kendra delivered the coffee and took a seat. Grey was studying the pictures on the wall and over the fireplace. "This is your husband?"

"Yes. That's Ronnie."

"I've never seen him at the coffee shop."

"No. He works out of town. He's on the road by the time you open, and you're closed by the time he's back home."

"I'd like to meet him someday."

"Absolutely." Kendra opened her Bible. "Let's get to it then. You're about halfway through the Beatitudes, right?"

"Right. Halfway up the staircase, according to Alex. I'm hoping you will help me understand 'blessed are the merciful, the pure in heart, and the peacemakers.' "

"Maybe you've figured out they are very much connected. Let's take them individually, and you'll see what I mean. Blessed are the merciful, for they will be shown mercy."

"What is mercy exactly?"

"It means forgiveness. To forgive or to be forgiven. It means not being punished even though you are guilty. In Bible terms, it means not getting what we deserve."

"Punishment for our sins."

"Exactly. Grey, a few years ago, my husband and I were struggling. We were both working on our careers and weren't taking care of each other very well. Heck, we weren't even taking good care of ourselves. That's when I met Pastor Tom at the coffee shop."

"I think I remember that day. I had just started to work."

"It was the day I learned mercy."

"How's that?"

"Pastor Tom helped me see that if I wanted to heal our marriage, I would have to forgive myself and my husband. We had to stop letting past mistakes, missteps, and misunderstandings interfere with our present and future happiness. We had to show each other mercy."

"Interesting. That was the day I forgave my dad, Ray. Stepdad, actually. I had blamed him for my mom's death.

It made me an unfortunate, miserable person. It hurt him, too. But I think it hurt me more."

"Exactly, Grey. The merciful will receive mercy. By forgiving Ray, you found peace."

"Well, I stopped the war, and somehow he forgave me. Yes. We found peace." Grey stared into her Bible for a moment. "So, what you're saying is when I show mercy and forgiveness to others, I will be shown mercy and forgiven as well? ... Is it conditional?"

"Think of it this way. When you don't forgive, when you hold resentment or anger, it's like a giant rock in the middle of your road or a clog in your drain. You can't continue your journey or eliminate the dirty water in your sink. You're stuck. Mercy is a step towards a pure heart and peace."

"Right. The next Beatitude. Blessed are the pure in heart, for they will see God."

"Well, if your heart is full of hate, anger, or sadness, it's hard for it to be pure."

"So, I need to empty my heart of the bad stuff to make room for the good."

"Your heart *and* your mind. If you are focused on God's will, your heart and mind will be filled with good."

Grey glanced out the window as she took a sip from her cup. "Yeah. I've been thinking about God's will."

"Good. I think it's different for each person, but I sum it up in one word - Love." Kendra allowed that to sink in for a moment. "God is love, Grey. He sent Jesus to us to demonstrate love, to show us how to love, how to *be* love."

"I get that, but some people are just plain hard to love."

"True. Think of it like this. Hating, blaming, or worrying about someone else is like taking poison yourself and waiting for them to die. The only one that hurts is you. Love is much healthier than hate. I promise. Remember, a pure heart is focused on God, *and* a heart focused on God is pure."

"So, I guess it's logical then that a pure heart is also a peacemaker's heart?"

"You're correct. You must make peace with yourself, the people in your life, and God. The bottom line, Grey, is if you want the peace of God, you first have to be at peace with God."

"Pastor Tom said I should stop fighting with God."

"It's true. God is fighting for you, Grey. If you're fighting with God, you're fighting with and against yourself."

"Ooh. That kinda hurts."

"I know. It was a tough one for me to learn."

Grey raised her hand.

"You don't have to do that."

"I have a question," she hesitated for a moment.

"Okay."

"How's your marriage now, Kendra?"

"Oh. Good question. It's better than ever."

"And your career."

"Same. Better than ever. I'm finishing my first book."

"That's your big project? Wow! That's great. What's it about?"

"Right now, it's about 215 pages."

"Ha!" Grey laughed.

"It's a love story. I'll get you a copy when it's finished." Kendra thought briefly and said, "Speaking of love stories, how is yours coming?"

"Mine? Oh, you know, it's in its infancy, I guess."

"That sounds like a start."

"It was a little rocky at first. I would say it started on the rocks. Fortunately, Nick is patient and is giving me time to 'catch up' to where he is."

"Nick is great. I think you guys make a great team."

"Thanks. I think so, too. We work well together, and the 'dating' is kinda fun."

"You'll get there, Grey. One step at a time."

Grey glanced at her Bible. "Okay, so the next two Beatitudes talk about persecution and pain. We start with happiness and end with persecution. I'm not sure I follow."

"Right. I'm going to let the pastor get into those with you. Meanwhile, you work on forgiveness, a pure heart, and a peacemaker attitude. Remember the great commandments - Love God. Love each other. That's the goal."

"More homework."

"Heart work, Grey. Heart work."

"I guess you're right. Thanks, Kendra. I'll get out of your hair so you can return to your love story. See you at the Barnabas soon?"

"Absolutely."

And you will be my witnesses, telling people about me everywhere...

Acts 1:8 (NLT)

Chapter Sixteen

Nick was changing the coffee filters. Grey was wiping down the counter. "So, how's the Bible study coming?"

"I'm getting closer to the Kingdom of Heaven," Grey smiled.

"That sounds like a good thing."

"Probably, but today, Pastor Tom will explain how I should be happy about being persecuted, insulted, and slandered."

"That sounds like fun."

"I'm sure it's just another step on the stairway to Heaven."

"Well, don't let me keep you. I can hold down the fort while you're gone."

Grey finished the counter and grabbed her coat. As she was leaving, one of Nick's customers came to the counter for a refill.

"I couldn't help but overhear. She's going to Bible study?"

Nick stopped to refill the empty cup.

"Yes. I guess you could say that. She's a disciple. I'm Nick, by the way. I don't remember seeing you here before."

"No. I was passing through town and came in for a cup 'o Joe." The stranger was dressed in jeans and a golf shirt. In his early twenties. "I'm Ryan," he offered.

"Good to meet you. Thanks for coming in."

"Sure. I'm curious. So, you guys are Christians?"

"Of course."

"And this is a Christian business?"

"The Bible verses on the wall didn't give it away?"

"I thought they were just decorations, like that cross around your neck."

Nick laughed.

"You've heard that before?"

"A couple of times."

"Has it ever been a problem?"

"Not really." Nick paused. "Sometimes people ask about it, but most times, it leads to a good conversation."

"I would think some people would be offended."

"That's a good conversation starter," Nick smiled.

"So, how's the conversation going?"

"Well, we hope not to offend. The Christian faith is all about love, peace, and hope. It's about people connecting with and helping other people. Most people don't have a problem with that."

"Hmmm. I thought it was about 'Thou shalt not kill, covet, etc, etc'…"

"There are some guides, mostly common sense, I think. Don't murder or steal. Love your parents. Love your neighbor."

"Can't argue with that."

"Jesus summed up the Ten Commandments with two commands: Love God and Love each other. Then he added one 'commission' to spread the word about God and the Kingdom of Heaven."

"So, shouldn't you be on a street corner, in a pulpit, or on a mission trip somewhere, as you say 'spreading the word'?"

"This coffee shop *is* my mission field. I'm spreading the word right now with my new friend Ryan."

"Oh. Right," Ryan blushed for a moment. "I get it."

"I'm glad you asked. If you want to know more, we have an informal group meeting here on Thursday evenings and a local pastor here every Tuesday morning."

"Thanks. I'm shocked you don't have people outside with picket signs protesting."

Nick laughed again. "Actually, we did. About two months after we opened, we had five or six people marching around the parking lot."

"What happened?"

"Well, we were pretty much unknown before that, and business was very slow. After a few weeks, we had a line out the door and standing room only inside. And that's not the best part."

"What could be better than that?"

"The customers started talking to our strikers. They bought them coffee and donuts. They took them umbrellas when it was raining. They told them what I told you."

"About love, and peace, and hope?"

"Exactly."

"And then what?"

"Those strikers are now part of the Thursday night group I told you about. They have felt Jesus's love and want to share it with others."

Ryan sipped his coffee in silence.

"Makes you wonder, doesn't it?"

"About what?"

"About how much better our world would be if more people started with love, peace, hope, and conversation."

"Yes. Yes, it does." Ryan took a deep breath.

"What's wrong?"

"I guess I've never really talked with a Christian before. You're not what I expected."

"Yeah. We get that a lot."

Be the Light

He comforts us in all our troubles so that we can comfort others.

2 Corinthians 1:4 (NLT)

Chapter Seventeen

Grey found Pastor Tom in the church library, a room filled with the aroma of old books and comfortable chairs. The lighting was soft and warm. She felt at home immediately.

"I didn't know this room was here," she exclaimed.

"It's one of my favorite places to be," breathed Tom. "If you can't find me, I'm probably in here, but don't tell anybody," he winked.

"It will be our secret," Grey whispered.

"Why don't you take that chair," Tom motioned toward a comfy-looking brown leather recliner.

"Perfect," she said as she eased in.

"Where shall we start?"

"Persecution and pain," Grey moaned. "Persecution and pain."

"Ah. Yes. Persecution and pain."

Grey opened her Bible. "Blessed are those who are persecuted because of righteousness, for theirs is the kingdom of Heaven."

Tom started to open his Bible. Instead, he closed it and took Grey by the hand. "Remember when I told you that the Christian life would not always be easy?"

"Sure. Bad things happen to good people. I get it. But ... persecution?"

"My first point is 'life is difficult' no matter who you are. Rich or poor, old or young, Christian or not, life is full of challenges. The good news is that we Christians have a God who loves us, a Spirit who guides us, a Bible filled with wisdom, and a community of other believers to support us. All of this helps us understand that whatever we are going through will work out in the end, exactly how it's supposed to."

"Wait, that's what Nick said. I think it was in Romans, it was …"

"Romans 8 verse 28."

"That's it."

"Now, let's look at Beatitudes 8 and 9."

"Persecution and pain."

"What Jesus was saying is that when you choose to follow Him, to become a disciple, there will be people who will disagree. Two thousand years ago, the Romans and the Jewish leaders disagreed to the point of death. That is still the case in some parts of the world. Where we live, the persecution is more subtle. It can be as simple as discrimination for a job, a promotion, or a club. Some businesses are sued or boycotted because of the owners' overt belief in God."

"And is this Beatitude saying that this is a good thing?"

"In essence, yes. It says that you will be rewarded when you share the gospel despite the potential negative consequences. And Grey, don't forget this important lesson: The very people we need to reach are those who might persecute or punish us. They need to receive the message of love, grace, and mercy."

"Even though they hate us?"

"Especially because they *think* they hate us. Remember what Jesus said on the cross. 'Forgive them, Father, for they know not what they do.'"

"Love your enemies," Grey echoed. She sat quietly for a couple of minutes and opened her Bible again. She read verse 11. "Blessed are you when people insult you, persecute you, and falsely say all kinds of evil against you because of me."

"Notice he says 'blessed are *you.*' He's talking to you, Grey. It's personal."

"Feels personal."

"Good. And verse 12 says, 'Be glad because great is your reward'…"

"In Heaven?"

"For sure, but often, the reward is seen sooner than you would think. Like, when a 'hater' becomes a believer or like what happened to the coffee shop."

"Barnabas Coffee Shop? What happened?"

"You remember. It was right after it opened. Oh. Right. That was before your time. You'll have to get Nick to tell you the whole story." Tom thought for a moment. "Bottom line, the people who wanted to punish him for opening a "Christian" coffee shop not only helped him but became some of his biggest supporters. Most are members of this church," he smiled.

"Okay, next, Jesus talks about Salt and Light. Are you ready for that?"

Tom stood up and pulled a book off the shelf. "I think the bigger question, Grey, is, are you ready?" He handed her the book. "I think you are. So I want you to read this little book, review your notes, and next time we meet, I would like for you to tell *me* what Jesus meant when he talked about salt and light."

"Just what I need. More homework."

"Heart work, Grey. Heart work."

"Right. Okay. I'll call you when I'm ready." She stood up to go.

"Perfect. I know you can do it," Tom smiled. "This is going to be fun."

Be the Light

I am leaving you with a gift—peace of mind and heart. And the peace I give is a gift the world cannot give. So don't be troubled or afraid.

John 14:27 (NLT)

Chapter Eighteen

It was a busy day at the Barnabas Coffee Shop, but that didn't keep Grey from doing some informal research. She was delivering a cup to a twenty-something redhead who looked like she had just finished a run.

"When I say 'salt and light,' what do you think?"

"Uh … pepper and dark, maybe? Is that my coffee?"

"Oh, sorry, yes. Here you go. So, when Jesus said, 'You are the salt of the earth,' what do you think he meant?"

"Do I know you? I mean, why are you asking me about Jesus?"

"Sorry. Again. I'm Grey. Pastor Tom wants me to explain salt and light, and I …"

Her customer laughed. She took a sip of her coffee and said, "Okay. I get it. Salt and light …hmm. Isn't this cheating?"

"I don't think so. So far, I have seven different answers from 11 different people."

"I'm surprised it's only seven." She took another, longer sip. "I think salt and light represent responsibility." She looked out the window. "Yeah. That's it. Responsibility."

"Well, that's eight. Just keeps getting better." She wiped off the table and turned to go. "Thanks," she called out as she scurried behind the counter.

"You've got to stop interrogating the clientele," Nick chuckled. "I need a flat white with a touch of cinnamon, please."

"Got it." She sighed, "This is not easy. It took a lot of work to get a one-word answer."

"You'll get there," he offered as he took another order. "Be patient."

"Right. My middle name is Patience, you know."

"Ha!"

Grey mumbled under her breath while she fixed the flat white. "This heart work is making my head hurt." She turned to Nick. "What do you think it means?"

"I'm staying out of this one," he laughed. "Medium cappuccino, please. No salt. Extra light, please." He gave her a wink.

"Funny. Very funny."

Be the Light

Whoever loves discipline, loves knowledge...
Proverbs 12:1 (NIV)

Chapter Nineteen

Grey finished her survey, did her homework, and called Pastor Tom to meet at his office. *"I'm sure he won't tell me I'm stupid, but it would be better without an audience,"* she thought.

"So, what do you think?" He queried. "What does 'you are the salt of the earth and the light of the world' mean to you?"

"Well, this has been interesting. It seems that it is very much open to interpretation. I have asked many different people, and the only ones who agreed were those who said they didn't have a clue."

"Yeah, but what do salt and light mean to you, Grey?"

"Well. Maybe I'm crazy, but I think they are about change."

"How's that?"

"Practically speaking, salt and light change things. Salt adds flavor. It preserves and heals. Light changes night to day, invisible to visible, dark to bright."

"All true," Tom added as he moved closer. "So what does that mean to you?"

"I think," she squirmed a little in her chair. "I think that as I progress through the 'stairway' of the Beatitudes toward God, as my faith grows, I am changed. I am transformed."

"Exactly!" Tom exclaimed. "And...?"

"And, as I am transformed, I become salt and light to others. My salt and light point others to Jesus and His teachings. Then those people begin ...or maybe continue... a journey similar to mine. They become a disciple, a student." She paused for a second.

Tom was beaming. "If I had a bell, I would ring it. You've got it." he said.

"One of my customers told me salt and light meant responsibility. Not sure I'm up for that."

"Oh, you are well past that, Grey. Your only responsibility is to be the light ... to let the light that shines within you shine on the people you meet, the people you know and love." Tom stood up and hugged Grey. "You are a natural when it comes to sharing. You are a great disciple. Soon, you'll be coaching others and making disciples."

"So, that book you gave me last time. The book about the seagull ... it has nothing to do with the Bible or Jesus or being a disciple ..."

"It's a story about getting outside your comfort zone. It's about stretching yourself, ignoring convention and society, and choosing a different path," he paused. "It's very much like being a disciple."

"Oh. I guess so."

"And one more thing. You're ready to fly, Grey. You are ready to fly."

Grey stood silently for a minute. "Wow. I guess I am a disciple now. I don't know what to say." She held her Bible as if to study it. She was turning it over in her hands. "So, what's next? Am I done?"

"Hardly," Tom said, his eyes gleaming. "You're on a journey, Grey, and you've just taken the first few steps."

"Where am I going on this journey?"

Be the Light

"God only knows Grey. I can tell you this. Your journey is your journey. It's not the same as mine, Nick's, or anyone else. It's personal, and only you can travel the road you are on."

"You are on a journey, too?" She asked.

"Of course. Every day, I learn something new. See something in a Bible verse that I had never seen before. I …" There was a knock at the door.

"Excuse me, Pastor, your next visitor has arrived."

"Look at the time. Grey, do you know Maria? Maria, this is Grey."

Maria was a petite lady with short, dark hair and deep brown eyes.

"You met her daughter on the playground a couple of weeks ago. Remember Mandy?"

"Of course. She's unforgettable. Glad to meet you, Maria."

"Maria came to us a few months ago. She started as a volunteer and now works part-time, helping to keep me straight."

"I'm sorry to interrupt," Maria said shyly.

"It's okay, Maria. We were wrapping up. Grey, keep up the God work. Read, study, ask questions, share. You are off to a great start."

"Thanks, Pastor."

She turned to go and followed Maria into the hallway.

"Maria, you look familiar. Have we met? Do you come to the coffee shop?"

"Oh no," she answered. "I can't afford coffee shop coffee…. I am just getting back on my feet. I'm blessed that

Pastor Tom has taken me in. I think he sees me as a project."

Grey laughed. "Oh, I think he sees everyone that way. It's a good thing."

"I guess so. I have a long way to go."

"Me, too." Grey and Maria walked in silence. She could hear the sound of children playing echoing down the hall. "Tell me about your family. What does your husband do?"

"Oh. I don't have a husband. It's just me and Amanda Jane. We were …"

Grey interrupted. "Wait, Mandy is short for Amanda Jane? That was my mother's name."

Maria stopped. "Oh."

"Did you know my mom?"

Maria blushed. "No. I didn't. Umm. I need to get to work. Excuse me, please."

"Sure. I need to get to work, too."

Grey decided to walk back to the Coffee Shop. She hadn't thought about her mother in a month or so. A rush of emotions took her by surprise. For a second, she felt guilty, and then she smiled. "I wonder how many Amanda Janes there are in the world?" She said out loud. "Such a cute kid."

Be the Light

The light shines in the darkness, and the darkness has not overcome it.

John 1:5 (NIV)

Chapter Twenty

"I met a lady at The Lighthouse today," Grey announced as she wiped down a table and threw the empty cups into the trash.

"Cool," Nick responded. "I guess?"

"Yeah. She's nice. Just started working at the church." Grey grabbed the broom. "I don't know. There was something about her. I felt a connection. She has a cute little girl named Mandy …Amanda Jane."

"I see." Nick waited for more. "I … see the connection. I think."

"No. There was something else. I don't know."

They continued cleaning for a while. Grey went to get the keys to lock up when she heard the tinkle of the entrance bell. She looked toward the door as Pastor Tom and Maria stepped inside.

"Grey. Can we come in for a minute?"

"Sure Pastor. We are all out of coffee."

"That's okay. Maria has something to share."

"Okay." Grey motioned toward the table she had just cleared. "We can sit here." She looked toward Nick, and he moved to join them. "What's up?"

"After you left my office today, Maria came in to tell me a story. It's a story you need to hear. I'm going to let her tell it."

Maria sat in silence. Her head was down. In her hands, she held a Bible. She grasped it so tightly her knuckles turned white. A shiver started in her hands, traveling up to her shoulders and head. There was a tear in her eye. She took a deep breath and looked up at Grey.

"I used to live here. Years ago. I made some mistakes, and I had to go away."

Grey looked at Nick, waiting as Maria collected her words.

"I told you I didn't know your mother, and I didn't know her. I did meet her one day, though. It was the day she died."

Grey caught her breath. "How …"

"Go ahead, Maria," Tom urged.

"I was just a teenager then—barely nineteen. I was living with a guy. Not a very good guy, and I had a baby. And I was high on drugs that day. Most days, actually. I shouldn't have been out but I took my baby for a stroll. I stumbled and fell. I lost control of her stroller, and it rolled out into the street."

"The street mom was driving on?"

"I was so messed up. I shouldn't have been out there. As I struggled to get up, I saw the stroller rolling across the street. There was a car coming." Grey grabbed Nick's hand. "It happened so fast. I was trying to get to her, but I couldn't. The car swerved to miss the stroller. It went off the road and hit a tree."

"She was coming to pick me up," Grey blurted.

"Pastor Tom told me."

"I got to the stroller. My baby was fine, so I went to your mother. She was hurt badly, but she was conscious. She smiled at me. It was hard to believe she was smiling. She handed me this Bible, and she told me to read it.

Then she told me to take care of my baby and to go, to leave her. I didn't know what to do, so I took my baby and left." Grey was in tears now. So was Maria. Nick put his arm around Grey.

"What happened next?" he said.

"When I got home, I opened the Bible and read about Jesus. I didn't understand but mustered the courage to leave my boyfriend's place. I left town that day and moved to a home for ... for people like me. They helped me get into drug rehab. It took several years, but they helped me get a job and taught me more about the love and forgiveness of Jesus."

Grey looked toward the door. Through tears, she studied the little sticker she had seen the first day she came to work. It read 'Forgiveness Starts Here'. She took a deep breath.

"How? Why? ..."

Maria understood the questions. "The Bible had the Lighthouse Church logo on the inside. It was signed by Pastor Tom and addressed to 'Amanda Jane, a great disciple.' That's when I decided to name my baby Amanda Jane, and I promised God I would return home one day to make amends for what I had done. I figured the church would lead me to you, and today, it did. I am so sorry, Grey. I ... " she broke down in tears.

Grey wiped the tears from her eyes, but they kept coming. "Maria, you have answered a question that has plagued me since the day my mother died. I have blamed my father. I've blamed myself. I even blamed God." She looked at Pastor Tom, then Nick. "I can't blame you, and I sure can't blame your little girl. Now, I know that my mother died to save a life. She forgave you. And I will forgive you."

Maria lifted her hands to give Grey the Bible. "No, it's yours. I want you to have it. Every disciple needs a Bible, Maria. That one is yours. You'll give it to Amanda Jane one day, and it will be hers."

Grey stood. Maria stood. Tears still streaming, Grey opened her arms. Maria fell into them. They hugged. Tom and Nick stood by in silence.

Be the Light

You are the light of the world. A town built on a hill cannot be hidden.

Matthew 5:14 (NIV)

Chapter Twenty-One

Two months later, Nick decided to try again. "Grey, more than ever, I know you are the one for me. I love you and want to spend the rest of my days with you. Will you marry me?" The mirror stared back at him. He blinked. The mirror blinked back. "Well, I'm as ready as I'll ever be. Wish me luck." He turned and walked out the door.

Three months later, Nick and Grey were married. The whole town celebrated. Six months later, they bought a diner. One Saturday evening, Grey was filling in for one of the servers at the diner. It was a slow night, and she was doodling on a notepad when a stranger came in. He was mid-thirties and nicely dressed. He looked like he had had a long day.

"Good evening, I'm Grey, and I'll be taking care of you."

"Oh, uh. Hi. I'll have a water, please. Do you have a dinner special? Of course you do. Whatever it is, I'll take it."

"Easy enough," she replied. "I'll get right on it."

After dinner, she approached with the check. "Everything good?"

"Sure. It was great," he reached for the check. "Do you have a minute, Grey?"

"Of course. You're my favorite customer."

He looked around the diner. "Looks like I'm your only customer," he smiled.

"That too. Hey, you smiled. I was getting worried about you."

"I'm sorry. I have a lot on my mind."

"Thought so. Me, too."

"What's bugging you?" He asked.

"Well, it's a long story."

"I've got time," he offered.

"Well, I guess I'm a 'disciple' in training or something," she paused. "My pastor says I *am* a disciple."

"Nothing wrong with that," he said. "Me, too."

"Lately, I've been thinking about making a change."

"Okay."

"When I was a teenager, my mom died suddenly."

"I'm sorry."

"Thanks. It's okay now, but I was angry and lost back then. My mother used to call me Abigail. I changed to my middle name, Greyson, and told everyone that Abigail was dead."

"Okay."

"Now, Grey just doesn't seem right."

"I don't know you, but you seem to be more colorful than "grey" if you know what I mean."

"Exactly. But I don't think I can go back to Abigail. Not crazy about Gail." She took a frustrated breath. "Oh, I don't know what to do."

"Grey, the original disciples changed their names when they encountered Jesus."

Grey closed her eyes, thinking. "That's right. I hadn't thought about that. Simon became Peter. Saul became Paul.

"And there were others."

"Cool."

"Change can be good for you, Grey."

"So, what should I change it to?" She pulled out her notepad.

"Well, you could pick something totally new. Something that has meaning for you. Or, you could shorten Abigail to Abby," he offered.

"Oh. Wow. That's funny. I hadn't thought about Abby." She put the pencil to her lips. "Hmmm."

"Well, I think my work is done," he stood up and put a twenty on the table. "Keep the change."

"Wait, you said you had something to talk about."

"I'm going through a few changes myself. Talking about yours has helped me. More than you know. Thanks."

"Really? You're welcome. What's your name?"

"I'm Kevin."

"Glad to meet you. My name is Abby."

"Good to meet you, Abby." He offered his hand.

"My pleasure," she said as she brushed his hand aside. "I'm a hugger."

"Thanks. Me, too."

"I don't normally hug strangers, but you don't seem like a stranger."

"Who knows? Maybe I'll see you around. I'm going to visit the church tomorrow."

"The Lighthouse?" She said. "That's my church. It's the greatest."

"Maybe I'll see you there."

"Maybe so," she smiled. "Goodnight, Kevin."

Nice guy, she thought. *I wonder what brought him to town.* "God knows," she said out loud. She cleared the table, turned off the lights, and started to leave. She paused for a moment to read the Lighthouse sticker on the door. It read, *Peace is Here*. She saw her reflection in the glass. She smiled, said, "Goodnight, Abby," and headed for home.

The Beginning.

Be the light.

Epilogue

Is there more? Yes, there is. It's your story, your transformation. The "more" is *your next step*. You've come this far; now it's time for you to take the plunge, start, or continue your journey. Pick up a Bible, open the YouVersion app, start or join a study group, watch *The Chosen,* talk with your pastor … or someone else's pastor. If you don't have a church, read *The Greatest Church in the World* and look for a church that matches your idea of a great church.

It doesn't matter where you are in your journey … whether you are a believer or not … there's no time like the present for you to receive the greatest gift in the world. All you have to do is ask for it.

The Beatitudes

Blessed are the poor in spirit. *Make room for God, and you will be blessed.*

Blessed are those who mourn *their sins and past life and ask God for forgiveness.*

Blessed are the meek. *Go to God in humility. He is your father, and he will give you strength.*

Blessed are those who hunger for righteousness. *If you want to live 'right', God will show you the way.*

Blessed are the merciful. *Forgive others, and you will be forgiven.*

Blessed are the pure in heart. *Remove hate, anger, and fear from your heart. Open your heart to God.*

Blessed are the peacemakers. *Make peace with yourself, the people in your life, and God.*

Blessed are those who are persecuted for my sake. *God blesses those who stand up for what is right.*

Blessed are those who are mocked or insulted because they follow Jesus. *You will be rewarded when you do God's will.*

You are the salt of the earth and the light of the world.

Also by Skip Carney

The Greatest Church in the World: A lamp on a hill.
Pastor Kevin is three hundred and forty-seven miles from home. Out of gas and out of options, he turns into a small town where he meets a pastor and a community that change his perspective on church success. There, he learns the principles that can make any church The Greatest Church in the World.

Available on Amazon in paperback and Kindle format. Also available on Audible. Read by the author.

Illumination: A Study Guide for the Greatest Church in the World
This guide was written for people who want to make their church great. It is a step-by-step guide designed to help discover the problems that need to be solved ... the barriers that are keeping a church from achieving its goals.

Available free in PDF format. Email your request to info@skipcarney.com.

Also available at:
***www.foundationforchristianeducation.com** or*
www.skipcarney.com.